A Bles from Above

Children are a gift from God; they are His reward.
—Psalm 127:3

by Patti Henderson   illustrated by Liz Edge

A GOLDEN BOOK • NEW YORK

Dedicated to Thomas—
you have filled our life with so much love and joy.
And to Noah—
the twinkle in your eye and your sense of humor are priceless.
And to Mark—
the cutest little caboose in the whole wide world.
We have been thrice blessed. Thank you, Lord.
And to all birth-mothers, especially Jean, Cindy, and Diane—
thank you for your unselfish hearts,
your unmatched gifts, and your courage.
You are an instrument of God's love.
And to my husband, Mike, my best friend—
thank you for your love.
—Patti Belling Henderson

To my loving parents.
—Liz Edge

Library of Congress Control Number: 2003107665
ISBN: 0-375-82866-4
Printed in the United States of America
First Random House Edition 2004

Once upon a time there lived a mother kangaroo who had an empty pouch.

Every night before she went to sleep, she prayed that someday her pouch would be filled with a baby to love and hold and care for.

One day, Momma-Roo went for a walk.

Along the way, she saw a pair of butterflies fluttering about in a field of flowers.

She later came upon a mother duck leading her ducklings to a pond.

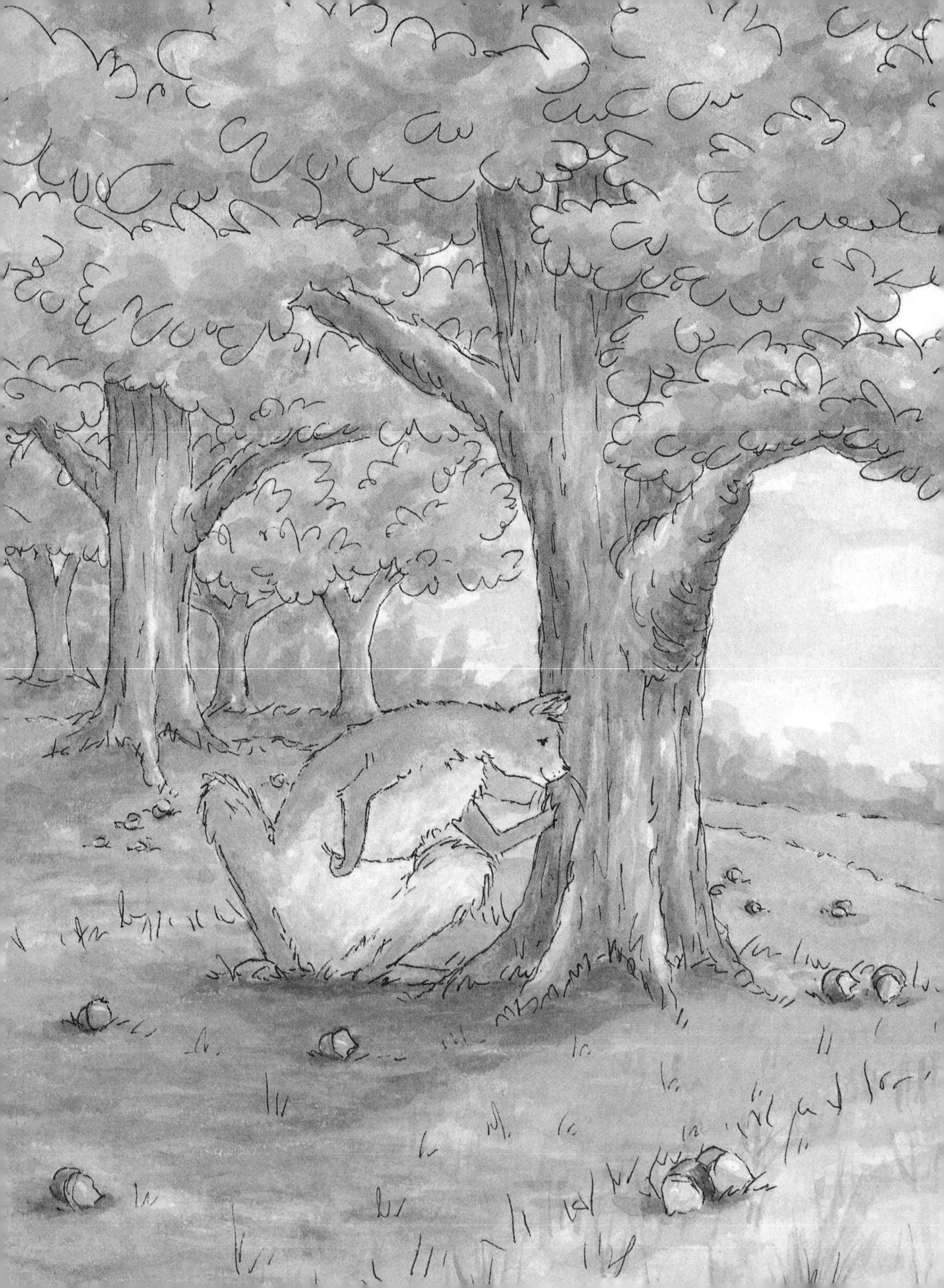

Next she spied a mama and papa squirrel
gathering acorns for their family.

She looked forward to the day she could share such wonderful sights and activities with a baby of her own.

Momma-Roo was getting tired. She decided to rest underneath the branches of a beautiful willow tree.

When she looked up she saw a bluebird nest stuffed full of baby bluebird eggs.

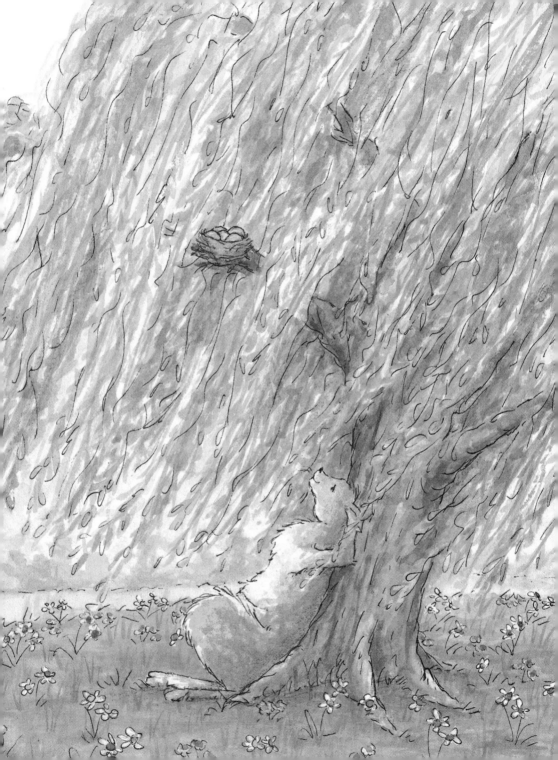

One by one, the eggs began to hatch.
The baby bluebirds stretched their wings and cried
for food.

The nest was getting very crowded.

Just as the last and littlest bluebird cracked open
his shell and stepped into this world . . .

. . . one of his brothers stretched his wings for the
first time.

Before the littlest one knew what was happening,
he was bumped from the nest and falling . . .

down,

down,

down . . .

. . . straight into Momma-Roo's pouch!

The baby bluebird peeked out from the pouch
and gazed up at Momma-Roo.
"Hello, Mommy," he chirped.

The mother bluebird looked down and saw her littlest one.

She knew her nest was not big enough for all her chicks. It made her happy to see her baby in such a warm, cuddly place.

"Hello, Little One," said Momma-Roo.

Then she hugged her blessing from above.
"At last! My very own baby!" she cried joyfully.
"I will cherish you and love you forever!"

On their way back home, Momma-Roo and
Little One frolicked through the field of flowers.

They stopped for a sip of water at the pond.

They shared grass and berries with each other.
They were so happy!

Now, every night before they fall asleep,
Momma-Roo and Little One thank God for all their
blessings . . . but especially for each other.

In love He destined us
for adoption to Himself. . . .
—Ephesians 1:5